THE SECRET
OF THE SABBATH FISH

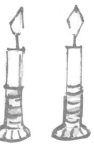

THE
SECRET
OF THE
SABBATH
FISH

by **BEN ARONIN**

pictures by **SHAY RIEGER**

The Jewish Publication Society of America
Philadelphia   5738 - 1978

THE SECRET
OF THE SABBATH FISH

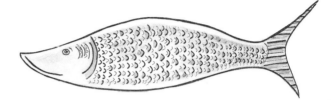

Tante Mashe lived in the little village of Barisev almost two hundred years ago. She was a widow, and not being blessed with children, she lived alone in her small wood-cutters hut.

Everyone loved her, and everyone called her Tante Mashe.

Small as it was, the little village of Barisev had a synagogue, and there the pious villagers would gather for prayer, for study, and for learned conversation.

There, in the women's corner of the synagogue, Tante Mashe
listened to stories about the great scholars and the great heroes of
the Jewish people. And as she heard these stories, she wished that
she, too, could do something for her people.

Tante Mashe liked to do things for people. When there was a Bar Mitzvah or a wedding, it was Tante Mashe's honey cake and Tante Mashe's sponge cake that the villagers "oohed" and "ahed" over.

From the little money she earned baking for the villagers, she put a few kopeks aside for the poor. Tante Mashe was poor herself, but there were others in the village who were even poorer.

One cold wintry Friday it was so dark that Tante Mashe had to light the little stub of candle to drive away the gloom in her hut. But she must save the other two candles, for in a few hours it would be time to light them with the blessing for the Sabbath eve.

As she looked out the window, the thought of what she had heard in the village this morning added to her sadness. There had been a pogrom in a nearby village. Cossack soldiers had attacked the Jews and had looted and burned many Jewish homes.

"Oh Master of the World," sighed Tante Mashe, "must I be lost in darkness without doing some little thing to help, to cheer, to strengthen my people?"

Suddenly, she heard a loud, hearty voice calling out near the window: "Fish, Matushka. Fresh fish."

Tante Mashe didn't heed the cheery cry. The fisherman called out in a louder, heartier voice: "Will no one buy my fish? Sanctified for the Sabbath it is, fresh from sparkling, joyous waters, with scales tinted like the rainbow. Will no one buy my fish?"

Then the fisherman opened the window and held out the most beautiful, gleaming fish that Tante Mashe had ever seen.

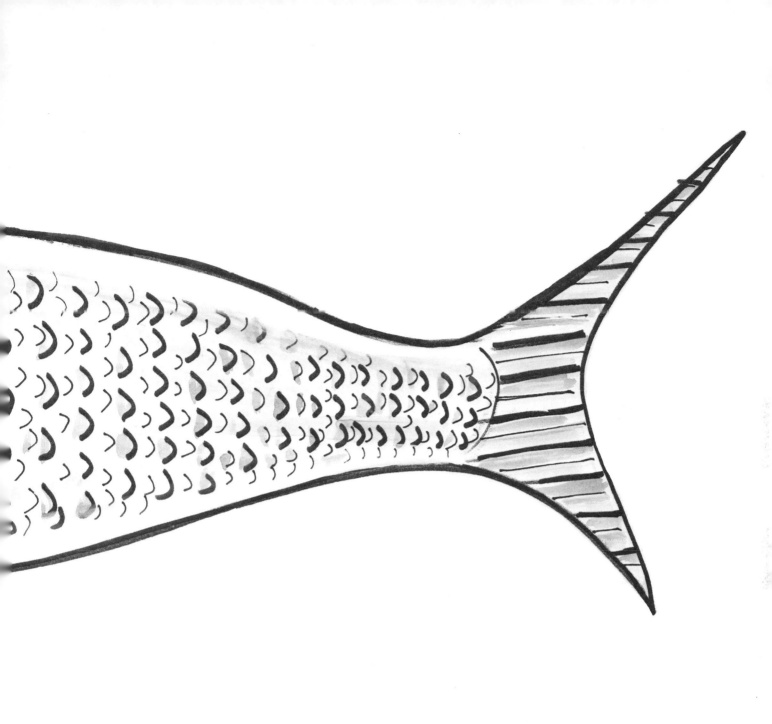

The room seemed to light up in the brilliance of the fish's scales.

Tante Mashe stared, fascinated, but all she could say was: "I have no money. Go to the others. They will buy your fish."

"No, little Mother, this is for you. Two kopeks. Surely you have two kopeks."

Yes, Tante Mashe had two kopeks. But she had put them aside for the poor, and they no longer belonged to her.

As if the stranger read her thoughts, he said: "What a feast this will make for the poor when cooked by your skillful hands."

"That's right," said Tante Mashe to herself. "If I take two kopeks and prepare a meal, not for myself, but for the poor, that will not be a sin."

She gave the fisherman the two coins and the prize fish was hers.

But what was the fisherman now saying in his ringing, cheery voice? "Don't fry it, Matushka. And don't bake it. But as you prepare it, think about what has been happening to the Jewish people. The fish will taste better that way."

And then he was gone.

Tante Mashe was puzzled.

What did the fisherman mean? "As you prepare it think about what has been happening to the Jewish people."

She took a large wooden bowl, and as she placed it on the table, she thought again about the pogrom.

The round wooden bowl seemed to her like a small world.

"I see," she whispered. "The Jewish people have been stripped through the ages, in every country, and in every part of the bowl we call the world."

She reached for the scaling knife.

"Our people have been crushed."

And she reached for the chopper. The wooden bowl shook under repeated blows.

"All this in a flood of tears."

She rummaged in the cupboard and found an onion. She grated the onion into the chopped fish.

"Onion—for the tears," said Tante Mashe.

"But through it all our people has continued to exist."
And she added the eggs. "A symbol of life," she said.

"Ah, what salt and pepper were poured into the burning wound of Israel."

And Tante Mashe sprinkled the white grains of salt and the dark grains of pepper into the mixture.

Thus she repeated the story of her people, emphasizing its woes. With every move of her fingers she patted the morsels, shaped them into balls, and put them into a pot of boiling water.

What madness was this? What had she done? The villagers would laugh when they heard about it. They would say: "See what the years have done to Tante Mashe. The years have made her a child again. She makes pies from fish instead of mud."

Ah, well, it was time to light the Sabbath candles.

Thus she repeated the story of her people, emphasizing its woes. With every move of her fingers she patted the morsels, shaped them into balls, and put them into a pot of boiling water.

"Oh, in what a sea of time were the Jewish people being prepared for their freedom! How the flames of hate and hope had set the waters of the sea of time, boiling and bubbling in turmoil!"

As she watched the pot boiling, Tante Mashe awakened from her day dream.

What madness was this? What had she done? The villagers
would laugh when they heard about it. They would say: "See what the
years have done to Tante Mashe. The years have made her a child again.
She makes pies from fish instead of mud."

Ah, well, it was time to light the Sabbath candles.

And, as Tante Mashe finished saying the blessing, an enchanting fragrance filled the room.

Now she heard footsteps outside her hut. She heard voices, the voices of the villagers.

"What feast is there this Sabbath? It is even as the Rabbis said, 'The Sabbath has a fragrance all its own,' and it has settled over our village."

"Yes, it is like the incense that Aaron, the high priest, offered upon the golden altar before the Holy of Holies."

The voices were growing louder, the footsteps nearer. They were at her door. Bewildered and beside herself, Tante Mashe stumbled to the door and threw it open.

The villagers came trooping in. There were greetings, noisy greetings.

And on everyone's lips were questions.

"What feast is this?"

"What strange fragrance, like the soul of the Sabbath itself?"

They crowded around the stove, and there in the boiling, swirling, bubbling water they saw where the enticing aroma of the Sabbath came from.

What a feast there was for the poor of the village.

"What do you call it?" a woman asked.

"Gefilte fish," said Tante Mashe. "I think I'll call it gefilte fish. It is filled with the history of our people."

"Tell us how you made it."

"Yes, tell us. What is the secret of this Sabbath fish?"

Tante Mashe told them how she made it.

"What heavenly being taught you the secret?"

The women crowded around her. She was treated like the queen of the village. Tante Mashe was beside herself with joy. And as she smiled through her tears, she told them the story of the fisherman.

And to the children that she rocked on her knee during the months that followed, she would tell the story, and at the end would whisper mysteriously to her wide-eyed listeners:

"And do you know who that fisherman was?"

" That fisherman was the Prophet Elijah."

ABOUT THE AUTHOR

Ben Aronin has delighted three generations of readers with his books, plays, and poems. His many books include **A Child's Book of Prayer**, **Birth of the Jewish People**, **Bible Stories in Rhyme**, **Jolly Jingles for Jewish Children**, **The Lost Tribe**, **Moor's Gold**, and **Cavern of Destiny**. An author, playwright, attorney, and teacher, and grandfather of six grandchildren, Mr. Aronin lives in Chicago.

ABOUT THE ARTIST

Shay Rieger is an artist and sculptor whose work has been exhibited in the Metropolitan Museum, the Joseph H. Hirshhorn Museum, and elsewhere. She has written and illustrated numerous books, among them, **Our Family**, **The Stone Menagerie**, **The Bronze Zoo**, and **Gargoyles, Monsters, and Other Beasts**. Her films have been seen on TV and have been shown in schools and libraries. She lives in New York City where her studio is adorned with her colorful paintings and sculpture.

"That fisherman was the Prophet Elijah."

ABOUT THE AUTHOR

Ben Aronin has delighted three generations of readers with his books, plays, and poems. His many books include **A Child's Book of Prayer**, **Birth of the Jewish People**, **Bible Stories in Rhyme**, **Jolly Jingles for Jewish Children**, **The Lost Tribe**, **Moor's Gold**, and **Cavern of Destiny**. An author, playwright, attorney, and teacher, and grandfather of six grandchildren, Mr. Aronin lives in Chicago.

ABOUT THE ARTIST

Shay Rieger is an artist and sculptor whose work has been exhibited in the Metropolitan Museum, the Joseph H. Hirshhorn Museum, and elsewhere. She has written and illustrated numerous books, among them, **Our Family**, **The Stone Menagerie**, **The Bronze Zoo**, and **Gargoyles, Monsters, and Other Beasts**. Her films have been seen on TV and have been shown in schools and libraries. She lives in New York City where her studio is adorned with her colorful paintings and sculpture.